# DUETTI, TERZETTI,
# E MADRIGALI
# A PIU VOCI

# RECENT RESEARCHES IN THE MUSIC OF THE BAROQUE ERA

*Robert L. Marshall, general editor*

---

A-R Editions, Inc., publishes six quarterly series—

*Recent Researches in the Music of the Middle Ages and Early Renaissance*
Margaret Bent, general editor

*Recent Researches in the Music of the Renaissance*
James Haar, general editor

*Recent Researches in the Music of the Baroque Era*
Robert L. Marshall, general editor

*Recent Researches in the Music of the Classical Era*
Eugene K. Wolf, general editor

*Recent Researches in the Music of the Nineteenth and Early Twentieth Centuries*
Rufus Hallmark, general editor

*Recent Researches in American Music*
H. Wiley Hitchcock, general editor—

which make public music that is being brought to light
in the course of current musicological research.

Each volume in the *Recent Researches* is devoted
to works by a single composer or to a single genre of composition,
chosen because of its potential interest to scholars and performers,
and prepared for publication according to the standards that govern
the making of all reliable historical editions.

Correspondence should be addressed:

A-R EDITIONS, INC.
315 West Gorham Street
Madison, Wisconsin 53703

RECENT RESEARCHES IN THE MUSIC OF THE BAROQUE ERA • VOLUMES XLIV and XLV

Antonio Lotti

# DUETTI, TERZETTI, E MADRIGALI A PIU VOCI

Edited by Thomas Day

A-R EDITIONS, INC. • MADISON

Library of Congress Cataloging in Publication Data:

Lotti, Antonio, d. 1740.
    Duetti, terzetti, e madrigali a più voci.

    (Recent researches in the music of the Baroque era,
ISSN 0484-0828 ; v. 44–45)
    For 2–5 voices and continuo.
    Italian words.
    Figured bass realized for keyboard instrument.
    "Texts and translations": p.
    1. Vocal ensembles with continuo.   2. Madrigals
(Music), Italian.   I. Day, Thomas.   II. Title.   III. Se-
ries.
M2.R238      vol. 44–45        [M3]        83–15218
ISBN 0–89579–191–9

# Contents

# Preface

## Duets, Trios, and Madrigals
## in the Early Eighteenth Century

In 1705 the publisher Antonio Bortoli of Venice issued a remarkable collection of vocal music entitled *Duetti, terzetti, e madrigali a più voci* by Antonio Lotti. The title is odd and raises some questions. Why, for example, are duets, trios, and madrigals—a strange assortment—gathered together in a single volume? Was there a demand for collections of this type? Why would a composer still be writing madrigals at the beginning of the eighteenth century? We can find many vocal duets written about the year 1700, but how are we to view these rare three-voice pieces? It would appear from questions such as these that the first words on the title-page (*Duetti, terzetti, e madrigali*) need some preliminary exploration before anything else is said about this publication.

Vocal duets accompanied by a basso continuo appear early in the baroque era, and in time this type of piece became, like the solo cantata, a popular genre of chamber music. At the beginning of the eighteenth century, when Lotti was working on his collection of vocal pieces, the duets of Agostino Steffani (1654–1728) were very much admired and widely circulated in manuscript copies. Steffani's duets—works that were not part of a larger composition, such as an opera or a cantata—often comprised three or more sections.[1] One of the middle sections usually had some element that contrasted with the other sections—perhaps a different meter or a different mood. Usually, the voices imitated one another throughout the piece. The duet for two sopranos with continuo accompaniment was a favorite combination, but other mixtures of voices were used as well. In a good many of Steffani's duets, the Italian text dealt with the complications associated with love, notably, frustration, fickleness, and torment. The popularity of these duets probably created a need for new ones by other composers, who, in turn, had to keep in mind the successful precedents that Steffani had established.

Someone perusing a copy of Lotti's publication *Duetti, terzetti, e madrigali* when it appeared in 1705 might have paused for a moment over the word *terzetti* in the title, since there was no standard literature for this type of vocal ensemble. Vocal trios are not easily found in opera or chamber music of the period.

The antique word *madrigali* in the title probably did not cause much surprise among Italian musicians in 1705, because all kinds of contemporary vocal pieces for two or more voices were called madrigals.[2] Some composers, such as Giovanni Maria Bononcini,[3] Giovanni Battista Bononcini,[4] Caldara,[5] Alessandro Scarlatti,[6] Stradella,[7] Steffani,[8] and, of course, Lotti, even wrote works that continued the traditions of the Renaissance madrigal. The singing of these madrigals, written in a somewhat old-fashioned style, may have even been fairly common in Italy during the early eighteenth century, but publication of such music was not. Composers probably considered these traditional pieces to be special efforts which would circulate in handwritten copies for the delectation of connoisseurs, not the multitude; consequently, only a relatively small number of manuscripts have survived. When Lotti included in his collection *recherché* pieces that recalled the style of madrigals written more than a century earlier, his contemporaries in Italy probably did not consider the music itself to be as extraordinary as the fact of its publication.

## The Composer

Antonio Lotti (ca. 1667–1740) spent most of his adult life in Venice and was closely identified with the musical life of that city. In his early twenties he sang in the choir of St. Mark's Basilica; later he became an assistant organist, rose to the rank of first organist in 1704, and finally in 1736 was appointed *primo maestro di cappella* at that historic church. For the city's theaters Lotti composed several operas—at least sixteen new ones between 1706 and 1717. Lotti occasionally left Venice. He once spent two years (1717–19) in Dresden, composing operas for the Saxon court. After his return from Dresden, Lotti composed no more operas. Oddly enough, this composer, whose career is associated so much with Venice, may have been born in Hanover, where his father was *Kapellmeister*.

Like many Italian composers of the baroque period, Lotti was musically "bilingual." He wrote operas, cantatas, and instrumental pieces in the fashionable idiom of the day, but he could also switch languages, as it were, by composing religious works in the *stile antico*, the severe style of the sixteenth century as interpreted in the baroque era. In addition to his fluency in the old and new styles, Lotti had no trouble, according to Sven Hansell, "adjusting to the 18th-century neo-classical taste favouring more clearly regulated harmonies and lighter textures. Perhaps better than any other composer of his time, he bridged the late baroque and early classical periods."[9]

Enough facts concerning Lotti's life are known to provide the outline of a brief biography, but the personal story behind those facts remains largely unknown. (Why, for example, did he stop writing opera in 1719 on his return to Venice from Dresden?) The one part of his life where the dry facts are enlivened with a bit of drama concerns his only work to be printed in his lifetime: the collection of duets, trios, and madrigals published in 1705.

In a letter dated March 29, 1731, and addressed to London's Academy of Ancient Musick, Lotti explained the circumstances surrounding the composition and publication of the *Duetti, terzetti, e madrigali a più voci*. The Academy later published his letter in a pamphlet,[10] both in the original French and with an English translation. Part of that translation follows here:

> The late M[onsieur] Marc Antonio Ziani, Vice Chapel-Master to his Majesty the Emperor Leopold, used from time to time to send me his Compositions; always desiring that I would send him some of mine. I sent him the Madrigal for five Voices, *In una siepe ombrosa* [i.e., *La vita caduca*], and he was so good as to cause it to be sung in the Presence of the Emperor Leopold. M. Ziani very politely congratulated me upon it in his Letters. . . . The Emperor Leopold, with his usual Clemency, ordered M. Ziani to acquaint me [sic] how well satisfied he was with it, and to write to me to send Him some more of my Compositions in the same Taste. I then finished the Pieces contained in the printed Book; and when I was upon the point of dedicating the Work to him, his Majesty unfortunately died. After his Death, M. Ziani, with the M. the Count de Par, representing my Misfortune to his Imperial Majesty Joseph I, his Majesty was pleased to take the Book of *Duetti, Terzetti,* etc. into his Protection, as is express'd in the Preface; and out of his Liberality was pleased to honour me with a Gold Chain, which was sent to me on the part of his Majesty.

Lotti's letter abridges the facts somewhat. From the available evidence, it appears that the sequence of events was as follows: Leopold I (1640–1705), Holy Roman Emperor and an accomplished musician, heard a performance of *La vita caduca* at court. Pleased with this work and its weary text about the passing of beauty and the end of life, he instructed Ziani to congratulate the composer and obtain more examples of Lotti's music. Lotti then sent the Emperor a manuscript collection of fourteen pieces entitled *Duetti, terzetti, e madrigali a più voci*.[11] The dedication to Leopold at the beginning of this manuscript is dated August 30, 1703; the last piece in the compilation is *La vita caduca*. The evidence suggests that Leopold received this manuscript collection, found great merit in the contents, and decided to subsidize its publication. But just before the work was finished at the printer's, Leopold died and the promised subsidy died with him. Lotti's friends at the imperial court reminded Leopold's successor, Joseph I, of the composer's unfinished project.

Quickly the subsidy was restored. Antonio Bortoli of Venice then published the *Duetti*, enlarged by four duets (Nos. [9]–[12] in the present edition) not found in the manuscript dedicated to Leopold. The dedication of the published version is to the new emperor, Joseph I, but it also makes suitably florid references to his predecessor, Leopold.

In putting together the original collection, Lotti may have consulted with Ziani about the type of music that the musically gifted Leopold and members of his court liked to hear and sing. In the manuscript copy of the *Duetti, terzetti, e madrigali* that Lotti sent to the imperial court in 1703, two of the eight duets (Nos. [1] and [8] in the present edition), all four of the trios, and the two madrigals call for a bass or baritone voice that is frequently doubled by the basso continuo line; possibly—and this is speculation—the composer intended these pieces for the emperor himself to sing.[12] Lotti probably did not have to make any inquiries to learn that Leopold, at least on one occasion, had publicly identified himself with the continuing tradition of the madrigal: in 1678 the emperor had accepted the dedication of a book of madrigals by Giovanni Maria Bononcini and certainly must have subsidized its publication.[13]

## The *Duetti, terzetti, e madrigali a più voci*

If Leopold was pleased with the quality of the pieces in the *Duetti*, he must also have been impressed with their variety. The collection contains compositions with two, three, four, and five voice parts; the two madrigals at the end (Nos. [17] and [18]) recall the works of Monteverdi and Gesualdo, while the other selections are more contemporary in style; some pieces (for example, No. [16]) give the impression that they are miniature cantatas in which the singers are performing a small dramatic scene.

Lotti's collection of *Duetti, terzetti, e madrigali* begins simply. Indeed, the first fifty-six measures of *Incostanza feminile* (No. [1]) might be described as a daringly casual way to open a work intended for presentation at the imperial court. It could be said that this type of plain, relaxed melody anticipated the more easygoing manner of the early classical style, but, of course, such an observation would not have been made in 1703. We can only presume that Leopold and his court must have been intrigued to discover that Lotti did not commence with something more imposing. By the middle of this first piece, however, the simplicity yields to baroque complexity. The remaining duets, often reminiscent of Steffani, take us through the assorted symptoms and images associated with love. Sometimes love is a matter of sighing and suffering, expressed in customary half-steps (No. [2], mm. 1–51); sometimes love's agonies are portrayed in somewhat extravagant imagery, such as the "drops" and "sparks" in *Crudeltà rimproverata* (No. [6]); *Capriccio* (No. [8]) begins by treating the subject of love lightly and almost comically (mm. 1–46), but this mood soon ends and the familiar Western idea of love as a sickness returns. There are times in these duets when the sound of the piece seems to be inspired not by love poetry but by the contemporary trio sonata for two violins and continuo (e.g., No. [11], mm. 31 to the end).

The four trios in Lotti's collection can be divided into two categories: (1) *Inganni dell'umanità* (No. [13]) and *Incostanza della sorte* (No. [14]) have no extended solo passages for the accompaniment or one of the voices and, for this reason, might be related to the *stile antico* tradition.[14] It is worth noting that these two trios and the two madrigals at the end (Nos. [17] and [18]) are the only pieces in the collection that do not allow the voices to rest at least a measure or two while the continuo plays alone. (2) *Fugacità del tempo* (No. [15]) and *Lamento di tre amanti* (No. [16]) have brief passages where the continuo plays without the voices and thus might be considered more modern than the other two trios. The texts of Nos. [13–15] all end by proclaiming some piece of worldly wisdom; No. [16] is about love. Lotti probably included *Inganni dell'umanità* (No. [13]), with its text about a warrior, especially for Leopold, whose reign (1658–1705) was marked by various wars and battles; in fact, when Leopold received Lotti's manuscript of the *Duetti*, he was in the middle of the War of the Spanish Succession. In all four of these trios, the bass and the basso continuo parts are virtually identical a good deal of the time; this occasionally gives the impression that these pieces are duets with an artificial third part derived from the continuo line.[15]

The madrigals of Monteverdi and Gesualdo may have provided the models for the last two pieces in Lotti's collection—the madrigals *Moralità d'una perla* (No. [17]) and *La vita caduca* (No. [18]). In these two works the composer observes the Renaissance technique of setting each idea or image of the text to its own music; at the same time, he stretches out everything with such baroque strain and intensity that the result is somewhat manneristic. Both pieces begin with slowly unfolding imitation and poignant dissonances; both end with elaborate fugal sections.[16]

Other than the two final pieces in the *Duetti*, Lotti's known contribution to the traditional madrigal literature consists of a five-voice madrigal (now lost),[17] which he wrote when he was in the service of the court at Dresden, and a work entitled *Spirto di Dio*.[18] This latter piece—for four voices, probably unaccompanied—was first sung in 1736 as the Doge sailed in the Bucintoro for his symbolic wedding with the Adriatic Sea. Because *Spirto di Dio* was intended for outdoor performance, the work has none of the intimacy associated with a madrigal and could better be described as an Italian ceremonial motet. No doubt Lotti wrote other pieces that were accompanied only by a continuo and were called madrigals (as is the case in Nos. [17]–[18]), but they remain to be discovered. Several

European libraries have manuscript collections labeled "Madrigals by Lotti."[19] Investigation so far, however, has shown these pieces to be either *Spirto di Dio* or excerpts from the *Duetti*.

The style of the pieces in the *Duetti* is reminiscent of music by Legrenzi, Caldara, and A. Scarlatti. Like these and other Italian composers of the period, Lotti resorted to mildly chromatic harmonies, especially when the text mentions the agonies of love. His fondness for sequences, especially near the beginning of a piece, is conspicuous. In the vocal parts Lotti occasionally used leaps of an octave or a seventh that call attention to themselves. (See, for example, No. [2], mm. 53, 56, etc.; No. [5], m. 43, etc.; No. [7], mm. 105–107; No. [8], mm. 103, 105; No. [9], mm. 16, 17, 21, 22, 27, 29; No. [10], mm. 48, 51, 52, etc.; No. [11], mm. 12–17; No. [12], mm. 162–163, 169, 173, etc.) Also, he could be exceptionally daring in his treatment of dissonance. The passing dissonances in *Fugacità del tempo* (No. [15], mm. 119–120 and 140–141) and the clashes near the beginning of *La vita caduca* (No. [18], mm. 5–6) are two examples; in neither case could it be said that the text motivates these dissonances.

Each of the eighteen poems in Lotti's collection—undoubtedly written by a poet or poets who understood a composer's needs—contains at least two different moods (e.g., pain, resignation, longing, contentment) as well as words that call for word-painting (e.g., *veloce* in No. [1]). Lotti, like Steffani, took advantage of these possibilities by dividing the individual pieces into sections that differ in character. Poems that end with some wise observation (Nos. [13]–[15], [17], and [18]) gave Lotti the opportunity to compose something fugal for these final words. If the words that opened a poem were repeated at the end, Lotti also repeated some of the opening music (Nos. [3], [7], [10], and [16]).

Neither the handwritten copy of the *Duetti* presented to the Emperor nor the printed edition of 1705 identifies the author or authors of the poems in this collection. Lotti mentioned in his correspondence with London's Academy of Ancient Musick that Pietro Giovanni Pariati (1665–1733) wrote the words of *La vita caduca*, but it has not been possible to identify any of the other poets.[20] Steffani, Handel, and other baroque composers all set texts that are quite similar to those in the *Duetti*.

## Controversies

The publication of the *Duetti* with a dedication to the emperor—tantamount to imperial approval of Lotti's music—brought the composer considerable prestige but it also involved him in two scandals.

A pamphlet printed sometime between 1711 and 1716 subjected Lotti's collection to severe criticism. This sixty-eight-page booklet, entitled *Lettera familiare*

[sic] *d'un Accademico Filarmonico*, pretends to be a letter from an unnamed musician who had been sent a copy of the *Duetti* with the name of the composer removed. Today, it is generally agreed that Benedetto Marcello, one of Lotti's students, was the author of this sly attack in the form of an anonymous letter to a nameless friend about an anonymous publication of 1705.[21]

Marcello began his criticism with general, philosophical comments on beauty, and then gave several particular examples of things that displeased him in the *Duetti* collection: the treatment of dissonances, the imitations, the excessive use of passages in parallel thirds, the modulations, etc. In brief, Marcello accused the composer of ignoring the accepted laws of composition and, hence, the laws of beauty. As an example, he pointed to mm. 150–154 of *Querèla amorosa* (No. [3]) where the voices begin each measure an octave apart or at the unison. Marcello, in addition, had no sympathy with the kind of melodic simplicity used in the first section of *Incostanza feminile* (No. [1]); he called it trivial and pronounced the whole piece "quite natural and easy-going, but lacking invention."[22]

The pamphlet contains about a hundred musical examples, including excerpts from Lotti's collection, "improved" versions of this music, and quotations from the works of other composers. Marcello's critical analysis went as far as the eleventh piece in Lotti's collection and then broke off abruptly. The last page of the booklet contains the following words, set in a different type:

> Resta imperfetta, e non pubblicata la Stampa per favorire (ad' istanza di premurosa Intercessione) l'Autore de Madrigali.

> (Let the printing [of this pamphlet] remain incomplete and unpublished (at the instance of an earnest intervention), as a kindness to the composer of madrigals.)

We do not know whether the pamphlet was ever widely circulated. Just one known copy survives, in the Biblioteca Nazionale Marciana, Venice (Musica: 1219). Perhaps it was the only copy made after Lotti or someone else had intervened.

Marcello's criticisms were probably motivated more by some personal grudge than by a philosophical concern for beauty. Nevertheless, he did open a debate and bring up questions that, unfortunately, cannot all be addressed here.[23] Was Lotti, for example, guilty of violating the laws of composition or was he within accepted limits? In what way are the different pieces in the collection "conventionally modern" or "old fashioned" or "ahead of their time"? Did Marcello uncover evidence of incompetence or of bold experimentation? It might help our sense of perspective in this debate to remember that Padre Martini, certainly one of the most exacting judges of musical quality in the eighteenth century, reprinted the last section of Lotti's *Inganni dell'umanità* (No. [13], mm. 49–95) in his *Esemplare o sia saggio fondamentale pratico di contrappunto*

(Bologna, 1774). Martini praised the composer and perhaps intended this, many years after the event, as a response to Marcello's attack. We should also keep in mind that, although Lotti lived for approximately thirty years after Marcello dissected the *Duetti*, none of his other music was published during his lifetime.[24]

A second controversy began in 1728 when the composer Maurice Greene presented a copy of the madrigal *La vita caduca* to London's Academy of Ancient Musick and claimed the piece was the work of Giovanni Battista Bononcini. It was soon discovered that the same madrigal could be found at the end of Lotti's *Duetti, terzetti, e madrigali*; Bononcini's supporters reacted by accusing Lotti of plagiarism. The leadership of the Academy tried to settle the matter by writing to Lotti. Letters went back and forth. Bononcini was also contacted, but he supposedly said nothing in his defense. Eventually Lotti assembled sworn statements from Pariati (who wrote the text), Fux, Caldara, and others to support his case. Bononcini's enemies then presented all of this correspondence in the previously cited pamphlet entitled *Letters from the Academy of Ancient Musick at London, to Sig[r] Antonio Lotti of Venice with His Answers and Testimonies* (London, 1732).[25]

Lotti's general opinion of the whole matter can be seen in his reaction to the news that Bononcini's supporters had withdrawn from the Academy over the disputed madrigal:

> I think, however, that they [Bononcini's supporters] do not so much consult the Honor of their Friend, because by separating from the Academy they show a Resentment which might be just, were the Dispute about an only Child, but for a Madrigal indeed it is too much, since Signor Buononcini [sic] can make others equal and much superior.[26]

The dispute, Lotti seemed to be saying, was being blown out of all proportion. *La vita caduca* was hardly Bononcini's sole claim to fame—an "only child"—nor, as we have seen, was it a unique specimen of an eighteenth-century madrigal. But protecting his authorship of the piece that had played an important part in advancing his career was, nonetheless, a matter of concern to Lotti.

One ironic point about this controversy over the authorship of *La vita caduca* is that baroque composers borrowed freely from one another. Certainly Handel, Bononcini's competitor in London, was a master of this. Acceptable limits on the common practice of borrowing were, it seems, refined in the Lotti-Bononcini case.

## Performance Practice

The voice designations given in this edition are those assigned by the composer himself. The tables of contents in both sources of this edition indicate the voices that sing each piece by using "C" for cantus, "A" for alto, "T" for tenor, and "B" for bass. At the beginning of each piece in the sources, the only indication of which voices are to be used is the clefs. Performers should note that although the tables of contents and the choice of clef specify a bass voice for Nos. [1], [8], [13], [14], [15], and [16], a baritone could sing these parts comfortably. In light of the complicated voice lines, Lotti in all probability intended the pieces in the collection to be performed with only one singer to a part. A small chorus, however, could be appropriate for the two madrigals (Nos. [17]–[18]).

Ideally a low instrument, such as a cello, should play the continuo line that Lotti provided (the lowest notes of the accompaniment in this present edition), and a keyboard instrument or a lute should improvise above that bass. But a harpsichord, with or without a cello on the continuo line, would be an appropriate and effective accompaniment throughout the *Duetti*, except in the two madrigals. For harmonic reasons it is important that the bass parts in those pieces be clearly audible. Thus, the support of a cello (or gamba or bassoon) will probably be necessary, especially if more than one singer is assigned to each vocal part.

The keyboard realizations in the present edition have been kept as simple and as unobtrusive as possible. The experienced keyboard player will recognize that the harmonic outline suggested here will need all kinds of decorative runs and flourishes. Sometimes, for the sake of variety or other reasons dictated by the music itself, the keyboard player should consider keeping the accompaniment thin and avoid the sound of a relentless succession of full chords. (See, for example, No. [8], mm. 1–28, where the playfulness of the music would seem to demand a light accompaniment.)

Lotti knew—indeed, he expected—that singers would also add all kinds of decorations to the vocal lines he had provided, and that they would make decisions on tempo, dynamics, and phrasing to suit themselves. Eighteenth-century singers interjected their own tastes into the performance of this music, and modern singers should do the same by adding the ornamentation and dynamic inflections they consider appropriate, in accord with scholarly research.[27] In fact, even the simple vocal lines occasionally encountered in the *Duetti* (e.g., the beginning of No. [1]) may have disappeared under layers of vocal ornamentation. While every piece in the *Duetti* needs some ornamentation added to the vocal parts, especially at cadences, a case could be made for adding only a small amount of decoration to the two madrigals at the end of the collection.

## Sources

There are two main sources for Lotti's *Duetti, terzetti, e madrigali*: (1) the handwritten score that the composer dedicated to Emperor Leopold I (and which is now in the Österreichische Nationalbibliothek, Vienna, Cod. 18776), and (2) the edition of the score published by Bortoli in Venice in 1705. The handwritten copy in Vienna (Wien) will be referred to as W, the 1705 publication as P. The present edition has used the copy of the *Duetti* in the Drexel Collection (No. 4273), New York Public Library, for P.

W, written in modern notation, measures 27x22 cm. The dedication is dated August 30, 1703. The initial letter of each piece is richly decorated, probably an indication that a professional copyist prepared this score. (See Plate I.) The fourteen pieces in W are listed below as they appear in the manuscript; each piece is followed by the number that indicates its location in the publication of 1705 (P). The present edition follows the order of P. (The four duets added to P are Nos. [9]–[12] in that source and in the present edition.)

| Order in W | Order in P |
|---|---|
| *Incostanza feminile* | 1 |
| *Scherzo d'amore* | 2 |
| *Querèla amorosa* | 3 |
| *Giuramento amoroso* | 7 |
| *Crudeltà rimproverta* | 6 |
| *Capriccio* | 8 |
| *Supplica ad Amore* | 5 |
| *Funerale della speranza* | 4 |
| *Inganni dell'umanità* | 13 |
| *Incostanza della sorte* | 14 |
| *Lamento di tre amanti* | 16 |
| *Fugacità del tempo* | 15 |
| *Moralità d'una perla* | 17 |
| *La vita caduca* | 18 |

Each piece in W has been numbered but in a handwriting that is not the original copyist's. On the first pages of *Inganni dell'umanità*, *Incostanza della sortè*, *Fugacità del tempo*, *Moralità d'una perla*, and *La vita caduca* in W, the word *Morale* is written in the upper right-hand corner; the texts of these pieces convey some kind of moral. On the first pages of the other pieces, the word *Amoroso* is in the same position, in order to indicate that the texts are about love. The designations *Morale* and *Amoroso* are lacking in P.

The edition of the *Duetti* published by Antonio Bortoli in 1705 is rather large in size (37.7 x 24.5 cm. in upright format). The diamond-head notation that the printer used sometimes makes it difficult to tell which syllable corresponds with which note. (See Plate II.) The following pieces in P do not appear in W:

> [9] *Amor, che spera*
> [10] *Lontananza insopportabile*
> [11] *Patimento in Amore*
> [12] *Cambio de' cuori*

The first signature in P consists of the four unnumbered pages that contain the title-page, the dedication, and an advertisement from the publisher about two of his other offerings (Carlo Marini's Sonatas for Violin Solo, Op. 8, and the treatise *Musico testore* by Zaccaria Tevo). This is followed by the music printed, for the most part, on signatures that consist of two sheets of paper folded to form eight pages. On the bottom of the first and third pages of each set of eight pages are the words "Duetti, Terzetti, e Madrigali di Antonio Lotti. Opera Prima," followed by a capital letter of the alphabet in the pattern A, A$_2$ (first and third pages of first set), B, B$_2$ (first and third pages of the second set), etc. A through Q are represented, except for J and J$_1$ which are omitted. The last signature comprises three sheets of paper (lettered R, R$_2$, and R$_3$), folded to produce twelve pages. The pages with music are numbered 1 to 140, except for pages 125 and 137, which are without numbers.

## Editorial Methods

All of the pieces found in this edition are contained in P (the publication of 1705), while all but four are contained in W (the hand-written copy expressly prepared for Emperor Leopold). For the present edition, W was chosen as the preferred principal source for pieces [1]–[8] and [13]–[18] because it generally has more detail (including more tempo indications and continuo figures), fewer errors, and ligatures which help determine syllable placement. The value of P as a secondary source for [1]–[8] and [13]–[18] is enhanced by its presumably representing the composer's later refinements, but it also shows many printing errors. P has served as the sole source for pieces [9]–[12] in the present edition.

In this edition, the order of the pieces follows that found in P. Neither note values nor meter indications represented in the source have been editorially altered in this edition. Continuo figures are those found in W or P; a few have been modernized (e.g., $\frac{5}{6}$ has been changed to $\frac{6}{5}$). The editorially added continuo realization is shown in small size notes. Incipits show the key signatures and clefs found in the principal source. Some original key signatures have been modernized in transcription by the addition of a sharp or flat.

As a general rule, accidentals in the sources have been applied to repeated notes both within and across barlines, but a rest or an intervening note of a different pitch generally cancels the previous accidental. In this edition, the modern convention of repeating accidentals after each barline has been adopted without comment; redundant accidentals have been removed, and cancellation signs have been editorially added without comment, as necessitated by this convention. Cautionary accidentals added by the editor are given in parentheses. Note pitches, note values, accidentals, tempo markings, and continuo figures placed in brackets and slurs that are dashed are not found in the principal source. When these editorial additions have the authority of the secondary source, mention is made in the Critical Notes. All abbreviated tempo marks (e.g., "Allg$^{o}$" in W and "Alleg." in P) have been spelled out.

The original spellings in the Italian text in W have been retained, with the following exceptions: (1) In W, "u" and "v" are written the same way. In this present edition, P has been followed to determine when a "u" or "v" is called for; in one instance, No. [4], "suenato" in P has been changed to "svenato." (2) In a few cases, P uses a more modern spelling than W (e.g., "aque" and "cattene" in W; "acque" and "catene" in P); in these cases, the spelling in P is used. In W and P the use of accent marks and punctuation is inconsistent; for this present edition, accent marks have been added or deleted in light of modern Italian usage, and the punctuation follows the sense of the text. In this edition only proper names and the first letter of each sentence have been capitalized.

## Critical Notes

All discrepancies between the principal source and the present edition that are not covered by the above Editorial Methods are documented in the Critical Notes, which likewise comprehensively report on variants in the secondary source. The principal sources are referred to as W (the manuscript presented to Leopold I, dated August 30, 1703, and held at the Österreichische Nationalbibliothek in Wien as Cod. 18776) and P (the publication by Antonio Bortoli, Venice, 1705). The principal source for pieces [1]–[8] and [13]–[18] is W and for pieces [9]–[12] is P. The Roman numerals I-V indicate the vocal staves numbering from the top of a system. The basso continuo line is referred to as b.c., and the standard abbreviations for measure (m., mm.) are used. The Helmholtz system of pitch identification is used in which c' = middle C, c'' = two-line C, etc.

[1] INCOSTANZA FEMINILE
M. 1, tempo marking lacking in P. M. 7, I, slur present in P. M. 40, I, slur over notes 2 and 3 in W. M. 47, I, slur present in P. M. 61, II, slur present in P. M. 80, tempo marking lacking in P. M. 92, tempo marking lacking in P. M. 137, b.c., fermata lacking in P.

[2] SCHERZO D'AMORE
M. 13, I, note 2 is a' in P. M. 28, I, note 2 is quarter-note in P. M. 160, I and II, note is dotted quarter-note in W and P. M. 165, b.c., fermata lacking in P.

[3] QUERÈLA AMOROSA
Title is "Querella amorosa" in W. M. 124, tempo marking lacking in P. M. 141, tempo marking lacking in P. M. 162, b.c., note is half-note followed by quarter-rest in P. M. 163, tempo marking lacking in P. M. 204, b.c., fermata lacking in P.

[4] FUNERALE DELLA SPERANZA
Title: First word is "Funeral" in P; same spelling in tables of contents in W and P. Text: "suenato" in W and P has been changed to "svenato." M. 3, II, note 3 is eighth-note in W. M. 4, b.c., figures lacking in W.

Mm. 16–17, II, tie missing in P. M. 76, b.c., figures lacking in W. M. 115, b.c., note 1 is B in P. M. 118, b.c., note 3 is D in W. M. 127, b.c., beats 3 and 4 are eighth, two sixteenths, two eighths (d, c, c', e, e) in P.

[5] SUPPLICA AD AMORE

Text: "ch'almen" in P. M. 28, b.c., note 5 is eighth-note in P. Mm. 54–55, II, note 1 of m. 54 and note 1 of m. 55 are c'' in W. M. 59, II, notes 1 and 2 are c'' in W. M. 85, II, note 5, sharp lacking in P. M. 95, II, notes are quarter, eighth, quarter, eighth, with no tie from note 2 to note 3 in P. M. 103, II, note 6 is eighth-note in P. M. 131, b.c., notes 1 and 2 are dotted quarter and eighth in P. M. 137, I, notes 3 and 4 are d'' and e'' in P.

[6] CRUDELTÀ RIMPROVERATA

M. 11, II, notes 4 and 5 are dotted sixteenth, thirty-second in P. M. 43, I, notes 2 and 3 are a', c'' in P. M. 81, b.c., ♯$\frac{4}{2}$ in W, $\frac{4♯}{6}$ in P. M. 85, b.c., bass figure $\frac{4♯}{3♭}$ under note 1 in P. M. 92, I, half-note, quarter-note in P. M. 115, I, word "e" is lacking in W. M. 116, II, word "e" is lacking in W; b.c., bass figure under note 4 is 6♭ in W; bass figure lacking in P. M. 121, II, natural sign in front of last note in W; b.c., figure ♯3 placed over note 2 in staff with eighth-rest over figured bass number in W; figure lacking in P. M. 127, b.c., 7 6♭ under note 3; figured bass numbers lacking in P. M. 159, I and II, notes are quarter-notes in P; b.c., beats 1 and 2 are eighth, eighth, quarter (d, d, a) in P.

[7] GIURAMENTO AMOROSO

Title: First word is "Iuramento" in W but spelled "Giuramento" in table of contents. Title lacking in P but "Giuramento amoroso" in table of contents. M. 72, I, notes are quarter, eighth in W. M. 75, b.c., note 1 is eighth-note with no rest in P. M. 82, b.c., figured bass lacking in P. M. 83, II, note is c''-sharp in W. M. 105, tempo marking lacking in P. M. 114, II, note 6 is eighth-note in P.

[8] CAPRICCIO

Title is "Cappriccio" in W. M. 16, b.c., tie lacking in P. M. 123, II, note 1 is dotted quarter-note in P. M. 126, II, note 5 is eighth-note in P. M. 129, I, fermata over rest in W.

[9] AMOR, CHE SPERA

P is the only source. M. 62, b.c., notes 1 and 2 are eighth-notes. M. 142, II, note 6 is a quarter-note.

[10] LONTANANZA INSOPPORTABILE

P is the only source. M. 22, b.c., note 5 is e-flat. M. 23, b.c., note 3 is f. M. 126, I, half-note tied to half-note.

[11] PATIMENTO IN AMORE

P is the only source. M. 7, II, note 5 is eighth-note. M. 26, II, flat before note 5. M. 105, I, fermata over rest.

[12] CAMBIO DE' CUORI

P is the only source. "Cuori" in title but "cori" in text. M. 18, b.c., note 4 is quarter-note.

[13] INGANNI DELL'UMANITÀ

M. 3, III, notes 11 and 12 are f-sharp and g in W. M. 6, b.c., notes on beat 4 are lacking in W. Mm. 38, 39, b.c., figured bass supplied from P. M. 39, III, sharp lacking on note 3 in P. M. 45, b.c., bass figure supplied from P. M. 60, b.c., figured bass numbers supplied from P. M. 70, III, eighth-rest inserted before first note in P.

[14] INCOSTANZA DELLA SORTE

Text: "apena" and "aque" in W. M. 42, I, note 4 is c'' in P. M. 46, b.c., note 1 is quarter-note followed by eighth-rest in P. M. 117, I, note is c'' in P. M. 148, I, note 2 is e'' in P. M. 171, b.c., fermata present in P.

[15] FUGACITÀ DEL TEMPO

Text: P uses both "rinova" and "rinuova." M. 30, II, note 4 is c''-sharp in W, b' in P; note 5 is eighth-note in P. M. 36, tempo marking lacking in P. M. 54, I, note 1 is e' in P. M. 112, b.c., note 1 is dotted quarter-note in P. M. 119, I, note 2 is dotted eighth-note in W; II, note 5 is g'-sharp in P.

[16] LAMENTO DI TRE AMANTI

First word of title is "Lamenti" in W but "Lamento" in table of contents and in P. Text: "string'il,'" "trass'e-gualmente," and "Ond'in" in P; "cattene" in W. Mm. 41–42, b.c., tie over barline lacking in P. M. 45, I, note 4 is quarter-note in P. M. 108, III, note 2 lacks accidental in P. Mm. 121–122, II, words are "come io dir nol so nol so" in P. M. 142, II, note 4 is c'' in P. M. 150, I, "seno" in P. M. 172, II and III, syllable "-te" lacking in P. Mm. 207–208, b.c., tie over barline lacking in P. M. 214, I, fermata over rest in W.

[17] MORALITÀ D'UNA PERLA

Text: "cingon'il" and "ch'anch'il" in P. M. 23, IV, note 3 has flat sign in P. M. 32, IV, note 2 is eighth-note in P. M. 59, b.c., beats 1 and 2 are same as IV in W. Mm. 59–60, b.c., notes are same as IV in P. M. 61, b.c., beats 1–3 are same as IV in P. Mm. 65 and 70, no double bars in W or P. M. 90, b.c., first note is a dotted half-note (g) in P. M. 105, III, note is flat in P; natural sign custos in M. 104 on source previous page. Mm. 115–116, b.c., tie over barline lacking in P. M. 120, b.c., fermata is present in P.

G. Francesco Malipiero's edition of *Moralità d'una perla* contains a number of unnecessary changes in the score.[28] Thurston Dart also edited the madrigal;[29] among the differences between his edition and this present edition are the following: M. 13, II, notes 2 and 3 are natural. Mm. 57–59 beat 1, III, transposed up a third. M. 105, III, flat not cancelled (which is the case in P).

[18] LA VITA CADUCA

Text: "quand'il" in P. M. 1, tempo marking lacking in P. M. 3, b.c., $\frac{5}{6}$ in W and P. M. 5, b.c., note 1, $\frac{5}{6}$ in P. M. 9, b.c., figured bass number supplied from P. M. 18, b.c., beats 1–3 are half-note, quarter-note in P. M.

19, b.c., no figured bass number in P. M. 20, b.c., figured bass flat over beat 2 in P. M. 31, b.c., notes same as V in P. M. 38, I, note 1 lacks accidental in P. M. 41, II, note is e' in P. M. 47, IV, two half-notes (d' and b-flat) in W. Mm. 62–141, slurs are those in W; no slurs in P but quarter-notes sometimes grouped together to indicate where syllables belong. M. 95, III, note 4 is e' in P. M. 96, I, note is dotted whole-note in W. M. 154, b.c., note is g in P. M. 180, II, beat 1 is quarter-note (g') in W. M. 196, I, half-note followed by quarter-rest and half-rest in P. M. 213, double whole-notes with single vertical stroke on each side in W and P; I and b.c. have fermatas in P.

In the late eighteenth century, Welcker of London published *La vita caduca* in a collection edited by Thomas Warren.[30] In that edition, I, in mm. 96–97 repeats "in su lo stelo" found in mm. 95, last note–96, II, except that the first note is c''.

The same added notes occur in an edition published by Ricordi in 1845 (Gazzetta Musicale di Milano, anno IV) and also in a later Ricordi edition (1930).

## Acknowledgments

I am extremely grateful to the following persons: Denis Stevens for invaluable advice and encouragement; Joseph Tusiani and Edward Williamson for helping me with my translations; Stephen Martorella for checking the keyboard realizations; and the staff at A-R Editions. My sincere apologies to them for errors that may have crept in after they were good enough to help me. Sven Hansell very graciously sent me a copy of his article on Lotti in *The New Grove Dictionary* before it was published. Most of all, I have to thank my wife, Mary Peckham Day.

Thomas Day

# Notes

1. Agostino Steffani, *Ausgewählte Werke*, Denkmäler der Tonkunst in Bayern, VI, Bd. 2 contains some duets and trios. The Recent Researches in the Music of the Baroque Era series will soon include an edition of twelve duets by Steffani: *Twelve Chamber Duets*, ed. Colin Timms (Madison, Wis.: A-R Editions, 1985).

2. See Frederick A. Hall, "The Polyphonic Italian Madrigal: 1638 to 1745" (Ph.D. diss., University of Toronto, 1978).

3. See his Op. 11, *Partitura de madrigali a cinque voci sopra i dodici tuoni* (Bologna, 1678), which was simultaneously published in parts (*Madrigali a cinque voci*).

4. Giovanni Battista Bononcini's madrigals are described in Lowell Lindgren, "The Three Great Noises 'Fatal to the Interests of Bononcini,'" *Musical Quarterly* LXI, No. 4 (October 1975): 564–565.

5. Some of Caldara's madrigals in modern editions can be found in *Antonio Caldara 1670–1736 Kammermusik für Gesang*, ed. Eusebius Mandyczewski, Denkmäler der Tonkunst in Österreich, XXXIX Jahrgang, Bd. 75 (Vienna, 1932), pp. 62–99.

6. There are eight madrigals by A. Scarlatti listed in Edward Dent, *Alessandro Scarlatti: His Life and Works* (London 1905; repr. ed., 1960), p. 212. They were recorded in 1975 by the Monteverdi-Chor Hamburg, Jürgen Jürgens, conductor. His edition of the madrigals is published by Peters (8243). See also his article, "Die Madrigale Alessandro Scarlattis und ihre Quellen: Anmerkungen zur Erstausgabe der Madrigale," in *Scritti in onore Luigi Ronga* (Milan and Naples, 1973), pp. 279–285.

7. For the locations of the many surviving manuscript copies of madrigals by Stradella, see Owen Jander, *A Catalog of the Manuscripts of Compositions by Alessandro Stradella Found in European and American Libraries* (Wellesley, 1960), pp. 56–58. Four madrigals, edited by D. G. Allen, are published by Oxford University Press (58.666).

8. Steffani's *Gettano i rè dal soglio*, ed. Colin Timms, was published by Novello in 1978 and was also included as a supplement to *The Musical Times* (February 1978); another madrigal, *Mortali che fate* is in the British Library, A 52–56 No. 77; J 83 No. 26.

9. For further information on Lotti's career, see *The New Grove Dictionary of Music and Musicians*, s.v., "Lotti, Antonio." The quoted passage appears on p. 250. Lotti's religious music is available in various modern editions; a facsimile edition of his opera *Alessandro Severo* has been published in the series Italian Opera: 1640–1770 (New York, 1977) with an introduction by Howard Mayer Brown.

10. See *Letters from the Academy of Ancient Musick at London, to Sigʳ Antonio Lotti of Venice with His Answers and Testimonies* (London, 1732), p. 9. The letters in this pamphlet, written almost thirty years after Lotti had sent his collection to the emperor, are a major source of information concerning the origins of the *Duetti*. The translation of Lotti's letter is printed in italics in the pamphlet, except for titles of compositions, which are in regular type.

11. This manuscript is discussed under Sources.

12. For other examples of baroque music for a bass singer whose part virtually duplicates the continuo line, see Heinrich Schütz, "Nachdem ich lag in meinem öden Bette," (SWV 451), *Neue Ausgabe sämtlicher Werke*, XXXVII, for soprano, bass, strings, and continuo; and Jean-Philippe Rameau, "Les Amants Trahis," *Oeuvres complètes*, III, a cantata. In Purcell's incidental music for *Timon of Athens*, there are two songs for bass solo; in both pieces the singer's part and the continuo line are very similar.

13. See note 3 above. Bononcini's collection of madrigals for five voices begins with one in honor of "Leopoldo invitto."

14. *Incostanza della sorte*, for soprano, alto, bass, and continuo, begins "Quel sol, quel sol istesso." It should be compared with a similar trio for two sopranos, bass, and continuo by Handel, which begins "Quel fior che all'alba ride." *Georg Friedrich Händels Werke; Duetti e Terzetti*, XXXII, ed. F. W. Chrysander (Leipzig, 1880), 100–109. Handel may have had Lotti's trio in mind when he composed his piece, perhaps around the year

1708. On the other hand, Lotti and Handel may have been following the example set by another composer, such as Steffani.

15. See note 12 above.

16. The beginnings of both madrigals are reminiscent of a *Crucifixus* that Lotti wrote for eight voices (SSAATTBB); the opening notes in the bass are E-flat, C, G (E. C. Schirmer: Sacred Music, No. 1192). This *Crucifixus* was once widely sung in an arrangement made for men's voices (TTBB) by Archibald T. Davison (E. C. Schirmer: Concord Series, No. 42).

17. Lotti sent this madrigal to the Academy of Ancient Music. See *Letters*, p. 21.

18. A copy of *Spirto di Dio* is in the Biblioteca Nazionale Marciana, Venice (Biblioteca di S. Marco, Cod. It. IV–1737 [in fine]). It was published in the Antologia Classica Musicale No. 6, Anno V (Ricordi, 1846). See also Edward Muir, *Civic Ritual in Renaissance Venice* (Princeton: Princeton University Press, 1981).

19. For example, the British Library, Bibliothèque Royale Albert 1er (Brussels), Sächsische Landesbibliothek (Dresden), Gesellschaft der Musikfreunde (Vienna), and Bayerische Staatsbibliothek (Munich).

20. *Letters*, pp. 6–9.

21. The title-page of the pamphlet reads as follows: "Lettera Familiare d'un Accademico Filarmonico, et Arcade Discorsiva Sopra un Libro di Duetti, Terzetti, e Madrigali à più Voci Stampato in Venezia da Antonio Bortoli, l'anno 1705" (n.p., n.d.). For a discussion, see Oscar Chilesotti, *Sulla lettera-critica di Benedetto Marcello contro Antonio Lotti* (Bassano, 1885).

22. ". . . assai naturale, e facile, ma di poca invenzione." *Lettera familiare* [sic] *d'un Accademico Filarmonico* (n.p., n.d.), p. 4.

23. For a discussion of issues that Marcello raises and other theoretical problems associated with the *Duetti*, see Gary Cobb, "Edition and Critical Study of Antonio Lotti's *Duetti, Terzetti, e Madrigali a più Voci, 1705*" (Ph.D. diss., Texas Technical University, 1979).

24. The signatures at the bottom of pages in the 1705 edition optimistically identify the collection as "Duetti, Terzetti, e Madrigali di Antonio Lotti. Opera Prima."

25. This is the collection of letters cited in note 10. The controversy is discussed in the article by Lowell Lindgren mentioned in note 4 above. For a description of the Academy of Ancient Musick and its history, see H. Diack Johnstone, "The Life and Work of Maurice Greene" (Ph.D. diss., Oxford University, 1967).

26. *Letters*, p. 19.

27. The amount of information available just on musical ornaments is enormous. See *The New Grove Dictionary of Music and Musicians*, s.v. "Ornaments" by Robert Donington.

28. In his edition, Malipiero rearranged the voices so that it could be sung without accompaniment. See his *Dieci cori antichi* (Boston and New York, 1928), I, mm. 14–33.

29. *Weeping, a Lover Languished* (London, 1959).

30. *A Collection of Vocal Harmony Consisting of Catches, Canons and Glees Never Before Publish'd to Which are Added Several Motetts and Madrigals Composed by the Best Masters* (London, n.d.).

# Texts and Translations

**[1]** INCOSTANZA FEMINILE

Al cor di donna amante
non si dia fede, no!
Che stabile e costante
femina per natura esser non può.

Se giura che nel seno
un Mongibel la strugge,
è foco di baleno
che veloce sen fugge.

Se mostra coi sospir
ch'il cor travaglia,
sono i sospiri suoi
fumo di paglia.

(Feminine Fickleness)

(Place not your trust in the heart of a woman in love,
no! For permanent and constant a woman by nature
cannot be. If she swears that in her breast a Mount
Etna is destroying her, it is a flash of lightning that
swiftly goes away. If she shows with sighing that her
heart is heavy, her sighs are the smoke of straw.)

**[2]** SCHERZO D'AMORE

V'ho detto tante volte, occhi tiranni,
ch'io peno, ch'io sospiro e no 'l credete.
Da me che più volete, o vaghi rai?
Con tanti miei affanni
sospirar e penar mi pare assai.
Mi contento di penar ancor, ma poi
per adesso non mi sento
di voler morir per voi.

(Love's Joke)

(I have often told you, tyrannical eyes, that I suffer,
that I sigh, and you do not believe it. Tell me, what
more do you want, o you lovely eyes? With so much
anguish of my own, to sigh and suffer seems enough. I
will be satisfied to suffer some more, but then I do not
feel I want to die for you right now.)

**[3]** QUERÈLA AMOROSA

Ben dovrei, occhi leggiadri,
come ladri del mio core
condannarvi a lagrimar.
Ma vedendo quei cari e dolci rai,
più che mai mi ritorno a innamorar.

E scordandomi il mio duolo
mi contento pianger solo
e non posso col mirarvi
benchè ladri, occhi leggiadri,
condannarvi a lagrimar.

(Amorous Lawsuit)

(I should well be obliged, charming eyes, as robbers of
my heart to sentence you to weeping. But seeing those
dear and sweet rays [of your eyes], more than ever I
return to fall in love. And forgetting my grief, I am
content to weep alone and I cannot, as I gaze upon
you, although robbers, charming eyes, sentence you
to weeping.)

**[4]** FUNERALE DELLA SPERANZA

Speranze mie, quanto infelici siete.
Già nel barbaro sen dell'Idol mio,
svenato dal rigore
per nostro duol commune,
è morto Amore.

Se vedere il volete,
nel sasso di quel core
sepolto il trovarete.
Sospirate, o speranze,
e poi piangete.

(Funeral of Hope)

(My hopes, how miserable you are. Indeed in the bar-
barous bosom of my idol, Love has died, bled by her
coldness for our joined grief. If you wish to see it
[love], you will find it buried in that heart of stone.
Sigh, o hopes, and then weep.)

**[5]** SUPPLICA AD AMORE

Amor, sepur ti duol della mia pena,
fa' che la Ninfa al mio desir rubella
o diventi pietosa
o sia men bella, onde così mi dia
se non maggior piacer men gelosia.

Ma se non vuoi far torto alla beltà di lei,
fa' che almen sia men bella a gl'occhi miei,
perchè di quel sembiante
io viva men geloso o meno amante.

(Petition to Love)

(Love, if you still care about my suffering, see that the
nymph who fights my longing either become compas-

sionate or less fair, so that she may grant me if not greater bliss at least less jealousy. But if you wish not to offend her beauty, grant that she be less fair to these my eyes, so that of her beauteous face I live less jealous or less enamored.)

## [6]  Crudeltà rimproverata

Se con stille frequenti
cade l'onda su 'l marmo, il marmo frange.
Se con faville ardenti
entra il foco nel bronzo, il bronzo accende.
Solo il cor di Mirtilla
al mio ardor non s'arrende e più s'indura
all'amor mio che piange.
Poi che fiera e crudel sempre egualmente,
non crede al lagrimar, fiamma non sente.

(Cruelty Reproached)

(If with frequent drops the water falls on the marble, the marble breaks. If with burning sparks the fire penetrates the bronze, the bronze ignites. Only Mirtilla's heart does not submit to my ardor and even hardens more and more to my love which weeps. Because she is proud and cruel increasingly, she does not believe my weeping, she does not feel my fire.)

## [7]  Giuramento amoroso

Poss'io morir, se non t'adoro, o Fille.
Ma che giova ingrandir co' i giuramenti
la mia costanza eterna?
Chiedilo a miei tormenti.
Dimandalo alle tue care pupille.

Ma perchè tu non vedi
la chiara fiamma ond'hai sì pieni i lumi?
E perchè tu non credi
ch'io per te mi consumi?
Torno a giurar la fè del mio martoro.
Fille, poss'io morir, se non t'adoro.

(Amorous Oath)

(May I rather die if I do not adore you, Phyllis. But what good is it to exaggerate with oaths my eternal loyalty? Ask it of my torments. Ask it of your own dear eyes. But why do you not see the clear flame whereof your eyes are full? And why do you not believe that I waste away on your account? I start again to swear the faith of my torment. Phyllis, may I rather die, if I do not adore you!)

## [8]  Capriccio

Voi che cercate Amore,
poveri amanti, io vi dirò dov'è.
Nelle guancie d'Eurilla, il traditore,
qual serpe infra le rose

già si nascose, ed essa il ricov[e]rò.
Credete, amanti, a me
che per tormento mio, purtroppo, il sò,
purtroppo, il vedo, e tardi
lo conosco alla face, all'arco, ai dardi.

(Caprice)

(You who seek Love, poor lovers, I shall tell you where he is. In the cheeks of Eurilla, the traitor, like a snake amongst roses he hid himself already, and she gave shelter to him. Believe me, lovers, that through my torment, alas, I know it, alas, I see it, and too late I recognize him by his torch, by his arrows, by his darts.)

## [9]  Amor, che spera

Tirsi, che fa il tuo core? Amando ei pena.
Di' che lasci d'amar: tanto non puole.
Troppo cara a gli amanti è la catena.
La fiamma donde uscì? Del tuo bel sole.
Chi lo strale vibrò? No 'l sai? Fu Amore.
O ferita gentil, beato ardore.
Che vuol? Pietà. L'avrà? La spera almeno.
Lice sperar pietade a la costanza,
nè mai senza mercè va la speranza.

(Love That Hopes)

(Tirsi, what is your heart doing? By loving it suffers. Say to it to stop loving: so much it cannot endure. Too dear to lovers is the chain. Whence did the flame come? From your fair sun. Who brandished the arrow? Do you not know? It was Love. O gentle wound, blessed passion. What does he want? Pity. Will he have it? At least he hopes for it. It is fit for constancy to hope for pity, nor does hope ever go without reward.)

## [10]  Lontananza insopportabile

No, che lungi da quel volto
viver l'alma, oh Dio, non sa.
Il mio core amor m'ha tolto
e lo diede a tua beltà.

Ahi perdita fatal, ahi rio dolore!
Vivere allor che in lontananza è il core.
Rendimi il cor, se vuoi ch'io viva, o cara,
o pur la pena amara
la morte mia sarà.

(Remoteness Intolerable)

(No, the soul does not know how to live, o God, far from that face. Love has taken away my heart from me and given it to your beauty. Ah, fatal loss, wicked grief! To live when my heart is far away! Return my heart, if you want that I may live, o darling, or the bitter anguish will be the death of me.)

## [11] Patimento in amore

Niso/Lilla, non posso più
soffrir la servitù
del dio d'amore.
Un interno dolore
il ripòso mi svena.
Un'insolita pena
mi va squarciando il core.

Amor, deh per pietà,
cangia tua crudeltà.
O s'allenti ch'io regga al duol che accora
o si rinforzi almen tanto ch'io mora.

### (Suffering in Love)

(Niso/Lilla, no more can I endure the slavery of the god of love. An inner pain bleeds my repose. An uncommon pain gashes my heart. Amor, ah for pity's sake, change your cruelty. Either allow me to endure the pain that grieves me or strengthen it at least to the point that I die.)

## [12] Cambio de' cuori

Duoi cori a me fan guerra:
Il mio che più non trovo; il tuo, mio bene,
perchè troppo crudele a me non viene.
Ma se core non ho, come sospiro,
come respiro?

Ah sì, dentro al mio seno
venne il tuo amor e nell'amarti io peno.
Deh pietade, mia vita!
E perchè senza core io non mi mora
con il tuo amor, dammi 'l tuo core ancora.

### (Exchange of Hearts)

(Two hearts are making war on me: Mine which I do not find any more; yours, my treasure, because too cruelly it does not come to me. But if I have not a heart, how is it that I sigh, how is it that I breathe? Ah yes, within my breast came your love and in loving you I suffer. Ah, pity, my life! And, so that I may not die without my heart loving you, give me your heart again.)

## [13] Inganni dell'umanità

A la tromba di Marte corre il guerrier
che sdegna della pace
il riposo ed i consigli.

E poi dentro ai perigli
sotto l'ombra dei lauri egli s'adira
e gl'ulivi tranquilli allor sospira.

Tanto è ver che nel verno è caro il verde
e sol si stima il ben quando si perde.

### (Deceptions of Mankind)

(At the trumpet of Mars hastens the warrior who disdains the quiet of peace as well as the advice. And then during the perils under the shade of laurel trees he grows angry and then longs for the tranquil olives. It is true that in winter, green is precious and only then is a treasure esteemed when it is lost.)

## [14] Incostanza della sorte

Quel sol, quel sol istesso
che sul chiaro orizonte
dalle porte dell'alba appena uscìo,
quello cui tanto piacque
empir di lume il mondo, il ciel di foco,
tramonta a poco a poco in seno all'acque.

E dice a noi che la terrena speme
ha così senza ritorno
l'oriente e l'occaso in un sol giorno.
E se nasce ridendo
dall'alba del piacer, ritrova in tanto
per sepolcro fatal l'acque del pianto.

### (Fickleness of Fate)

(That very sun, which on the clear horizon has but now emerged from the gates of dawn, the same one that so much yearned to fill the world with light, the sky with fire, sinks bit by bit in the bosom of the waters. And it tells us that earthly hope thus has without a return a sunrise and a sunset in just one day. And even though it is born out of the dawn of pleasure, it finds at the same time its inevitable grave in the waters of weeping.)

## [15] Fugacità del tempo

Fugge dal fonte al fiume il rio veloce
e per secreta via.
Torna l'acqua natia dal fiume al fonte
e per secreta via.
Perde la selva e 'l monte
quelle frondi e quell'erbe onde s'adorna;
ma poi nel maggio a verdeggiar ritorna.
Tramonta il sole e pur rinova i rai
ma il tempo che sen va non torna mai.

### (Time Flies)

(The fast brook rushes from the source and by a secret way. The water originating at the brook returns to the source and by a secret way. The forest and mountain lose those branches and grasses with which they are adorned; but then in May they turn green once more. The sun sets and yet renews its rays, but time, which passes away, never returns.)

## [16] Lamento di tre amanti

Ci stringe il core Amor con tre catene.
La mia da un labro uscì.
Un sen la mia formò.
La mia d'un guardo fu
che ci trasse egualmente in servitù.

Io per le voci amene,
Io per un sen di neve,
Io per due luci belle,
ardo ben sì, ma come io dir no 'l so,
e fu cagion di quella fiamma ond'ardo.

Un bel labro,
un bel seno,
un caro guardo.
Onde in eguali pene
ci stringe il core Amor con tre catene.

(Lament of Three Lovers)

(Love binds our heart with three chains. Mine from a lip came out. Mine a bosom. Mine was a face that drew us equally into servitude. I for delightful words, I for a snowy breast, I for two lovely eyes am burning, yes, but how I cannot say, nor do I know the reason for that flame from which I burn. A fair lip, a fair bosom, a dear face. Whence in equal punishments love tied our heart with three chains.)

## [17] Moralità d'una perla

Piange l'amante ucciso.
La foriera del sol, l'alba vermiglia,
è un'avida conchiglia.

Le lagrime raccoglie, onde ne forma
candida perla e vaga,
di cui n'ornano i regi
le corone regali e pretiose,
di cui cingono il collo
le donzelle vezzose.

Ed io rifletto intanto
che anche il fasto mortal nasce dal pianto.

(Morality of a Pearl)

(The lover weeps, slain. The messenger of the sun, the vermilion dawn, is a greedy shell. It gathers the tears, from which it forms a pearl, white and lovely, with which kings decorate their crowns, royal and precious, with which graceful maidens surround their necks. And I, meanwhile, ponder that even mortal grandeur is born out of tears.)

## [18] La vita caduca

In una siepe ombrosa,
quando il sol co' suoi raggi i monti indora,
pompa ed onor' di flora apre il bel seno,
una vermiglia rosa.

Ma le foglie odorate e porporine
circondano le spine
e cade in su' lo stelo
con pallide agonie,
quando de' lumi il re parte dal cielo.

Quindi ben lasso apprendo,
che terrena beltà simile a un fiore
circondata da pene
con effimera vita e langue e more.

(The Transitory Life)

(By a shady hedge, when the sun with its rays gilds the mountains, a vermilion rose, the splendor and glory of flowers, opens its beautiful bosom. But the leaves, fragrant and purple, surround the thorns, and the stem falls upon itself with pale agonies, when the king of lights leaves the sky. Therefore, quite weary I learn that earthly beauty, like a flower surrounded by suffering in its transient life, both languishes and dies.)

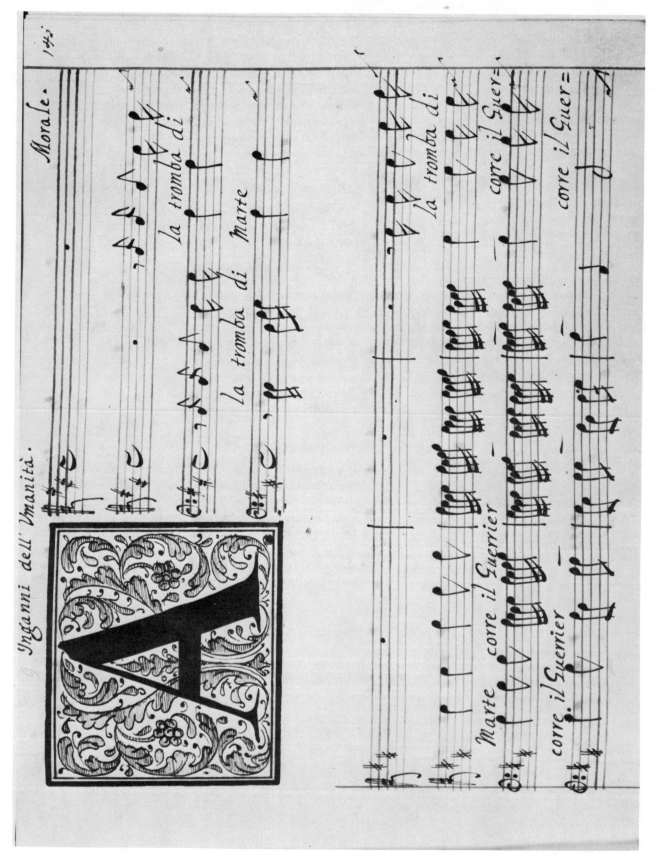

Plate I. Antonio Lotti, "Inganni dell'umanità," from his *Duetti, terzetti, e madrigali a più voci*, in the copy presented to the Emperor Leopold I. Vienna: Österreichische Nationalbibliothek, Cod. 18776, 27×22 cm.

Plate II. Antonio Lotti, "Inganni dell'umanità," from his *Duetti, terzetti, e madrigali a più voci* (Venice: Bortoli, 1705) Courtesy of the Drexel Collection, Music Division. The New York Public Library at Lincoln Center; Astor, Lenox and Tilden Foundations. 37.7 x 24.5 cm.

# DUETTI, TERZETTI,
# E MADRIGALI
# A PIU VOCI

# [1] Incostanza feminile

Amoroso

fu- mo, fu- mo di pa- - - - - glia, ___ di pa- glia, fu- mo, fu- mo, fu- mo di pa- glia, di pa- glia, fu- mo di pa- glia, di pa- glia.

glia, ___ di pa- glia, fu- mo, fu- mo, fu- mo di pa- glia, fu- mo di pa- glia, di pa- glia.

# [2] Scherzo d'amore

Amoroso

e no'l cre- de- te, no'l cre- de- te. Da me che più vo-

-spi- ro e no'l cre- de- te.

**Adagio**

-le- te, o va- ghi rai? Con tan- ti miei af- fan- ni so- spi-

Da me che più vo- le- te, o va- ghi rai? Con tan- ti miei af- fan- ni so- spi-

**Adagio**

**Allegro** **Adagio**

-rar e pe- nar mi pa-re as-sai, mi pa- re as-sa- i. Con tan- ti miei af-

-rar e pe- nar mi pa-re as- sai, mi pa-re as-sa- i. Con tan- ti miei af-

**Allegro** **Adagio**

**Allegro**

-fan- ni so- spi- rar e pe- nar mi pa-re as- sai, so- spi-

-fan- ni so- spi- rar e pe- nar mi pa-re as-sai, so- spi-rar

**Allegro**

12

14

-ler mo- rir per voi, non mi sen- to mo- rir per___ vo- i.

di vo- ler mo- rir per voi, mo- rir per___ vo- i, di vo-

Mi con- ten- to di pe- nar an- cor,

-ler mo- rir per voi. Mi con- ten- to di pe-

ma poi per a- des- so___ non mi sen- to di vo-

-nar an- cor, ma poi per a- des- so___ non mi sen- to,

-ler mo- rir per voi, non mi sen- to mo- rir per___ vo- i,

non mi sen- to di vo- ler mo- rir per voi, mo- rir per___ vo- i, non mi

15

# [3] Querèla amorosa

Amoroso

Ben do- vrei, oc- chi leg-

Ben do- vrei, oc- chi leg- gia- dri,

- gia- dri, co- me la- dri _____ del mio _____

co- me la- dri _____ del mio _____ co- re,

co- re, co- me_ la- dri del mio _____ co- re, del mio _____

co- me_ la- dri del mio _____ co- re, del mio _____ co-

a_____ la- gri- mar, con- dan- nar- via

a_____ la- gri- mar, con- dan- nar- via

la- gri- mar,_____ a_____ la- gri- mar.

la- gri- mar,_____ a_____ la- gri- mar.

Ma ve- den- do quei ca- ri, ca- ri_e dol- ci

# [4] Funerale della speranza
## Amoroso

# [5] Supplica ad Amore

Amoroso

34

on-de co-sì mi di- a, men ge- lo- si- a, se non mag- gior pia- cer, mag- gior pia-cer

on- de co-sì mi di- a se non mag- gior pia- cer                    men

men ge- lo- si- a, men ge- lo- si- a, men ge- lo- si-

ge- lo- si- a, men ge- lo- si- a, men ge- lo- si-

-a, men ge- lo- si- a, men ge- lo- si- a, se non mag-gior pia-cer men ge-

-a, men ge- lo- si- a, se non mag-gior pia- cer men ge- lo-

- lo- si- a.                    Ma se non vuoi_ far

- si- a.

39

gl'oc- chi mie- i,

gl'oc- chi ___ mie- i,

per-chè di quel sem- bian- te io vi- va men _ ge- lo- so _____ o me- no a-man-

per-

- te, per- chè di quel sem- bian- te io

-chè di quel sem- bian- te io vi- va men _ ge- lo- so _____ o me- - no a-man- te,

vi- va men _ ge- lo- so me- no a-man- te, per-chè di quel sem-

per-chè di quel sem- bian- te io vi- va men _ ge- lo-

42

# [6] Crudeltà rimproverata

Amoroso

44

45

48

54

ma_____ non sen- te, non

ma_____ non sen- te, non

cre- de al la- gri- mar, al la- gri- mar,_____ fiam-

cre- de al la- gri- mar, al la- gri- mar,_____ fiam-

- ma_____ non sen- te, fiam- ma non sen- te.

- ma_____ non sen- te, fiam- ma non sen- te.

# [7] Giuramento amoroso

Amoroso

Pos-s'io mo- rir, se non t'a- do- ro, o

Pos-s'io mo- rir, se non t'a- do- ro, o Fil- le, se non t'a-

Fil- le. Pos-s'io mo- rir, se non t'a-do- ro, se non t'a-do-ro, o Fil-

-do-ro, o Fil- le. Pos-s'io mo- rir, se non t'a- do- ro, se non t'a- do- ro, t'a-do- ro, o Fil-

-le, se non t'a do- ro, o Fil- le.

-le, se non t'a- do- ro, o Fil- le.

# [8] Capriccio

Amoroso

64

# [9] Amor, che spera

senza mer- cè va____ la spe- ran-

nè____ mai sen- za mer- cè va____ la spe- ran-

- za, va____ la spe- ran- - -

- - - - -

- za.

- za.

# [10] Lontananza insopportabile

Ren-di-mi il cor, se vuoi, se vuoi ch'io vi-va, o ca- ra, o pur la pe-na a- ma- ra la

-ra, o pur la pe-na a- ma- ra la mor-te mia sa-

mor-te mia sa- rà, la mor-te— mia sa- rà, o pur la pe-na a-

-rà, — mia sa- rà, la mor-te— mia sa- rà. Ren-di-mi il cor, se vuoi, se vuoi ch'io vi- va, o —

-ma- ra, ren-di-mi il cor, se vuoi, se vuoi ch'io vi- va, o —

ca- ra, o pur la pe-na a-ma- ra la mor- te, la mor-

ca- ra, o pur la pe-na a-ma- ra, o

-te mia sa-rà, o pur la pe-na a-ma- ra, o pur la pe-na a-ma-

pur la pe-na a-ma- ra la mor-te mia sa- rà, la mor-te mia sa- rà,

-ra la mor-te mia sa- rà, la mor- te, la mor-te mia sa- rà. Ren-di-mi il cor, se

la mor- te mia sa-rà, o pur la pe-na a-ma- ra la

vuoi, se vuoi ch'io vi- va, o ca- ra, o pur la pe-na a- ma- ra la

mor-te mia sa-rà, la mor- te, la mor- te_____ mia sa-rà.

mor-te mia sa-rà, la mor- te, la mor- te_____ mia sa-rà.

No, che lun- gi da quel vol- to vi- ver

No, che lun- gi da quel vol- to vi- ver l'al-

# [11] Patimento in Amore

88

# [12] Cambio de' cuori

Duoi co- ri̲a me fan guer-

Duoi

co- ri̲a me fan guer- ra,  a me fan guer-

trop- po cru-de- le, per-chè trop- po cru-de- le a me non

-le, per-chè trop- po cru-de- le a me non vie- ne,_____

vie- - - ne, a me non vie-

____ a me non vie- - - ne, a me non vie-

-ne, per-chè trop- po cru-de- -le a me, a me__ non__ vie-

-ne, per-chè trop- po cru-de- le a me,_____ a me non vie-

-ne. Ma se

-ne.

# [13] Inganni dell'umanità
## Morale

# [14] Incostanza della sorte
## Morale

Quel sol, _____ quel sol i-stes- so che sul chia- ro o ri-

Quel sol, _____ quel sol i- stes- so che sul

Quel sol, _____

-zon- te, che sul chia- ro o ri-

chia- ro o ri- zon-

125

# [15] Fugacità del tempo
## Morale

# [16] Lamento di tre amanti

Amoroso

Ci strin-ge il co-re A- mor, ci strin-ge il co-re A- mor,

Ci strin-ge il co-re A- mor, ci strin-ge il

Ci strin-ge il co-re A-

ci strin-ge il co-re A- mor con tre ca- te- -

co-re A- mor, A- - mor, ci strin- ge con tre ca- te-

-mor, A- - mor, ci strin- ge con tre ca- te-

- scì, da un la - - - - bro, da un la - brou - scì.

Un sen la mia for - mò, _____

_____ la mia for - mò.

La mia d'un guar - do

io per le vo- ci a- me- ne,

io per un sen di ne- ve,

bel- le, io per due lu- ci

**Allegro**

ar- do ben sì, ma co- me io dir no'l

bel- le, ar- do ben sì, ma co- me io dir no'l so, io dir no'l so,

**Allegro**

ar- do ben sì, ma co- me

so, io dir no'l so, io dir no'l so, ma co- me, ar- do ben sì, ma

io dir no'l so, ar- do ben sì, ma co- me io dir no'l so, io dir no'l

153

# [17] Moralità d'una perla
## Morale

174

# [18] La vita caduca

## Morale

Pietro Giovanni Pariati

[6]

188